I AM A MOUSE

I AM A MOUSE

BY HERBERT COGGINS

ILLUSTRATED BY JUDITH BROOK

ABELARD-SCHUMAN
London & New York

Library of Congress Catalog Card Number: 59-6671

For my sister
EDITH

Printed in the United States of America

I AM A MOUSE

1

I am a mouse. I might truly say a rather remarkable mouse. In the first place, I have no brothers and sisters. This state of affairs is very unusual in a mouse family. Also, I am very large for my age. When I was born, and father saw me for the first time, he exclaimed:

"Why, he's not a mouse at all; he's a moose." After a little reflection, he continued, "That's what we'll call him. Instead of Mose Mouse, Jr., we'll name him Moose. It will be easy to remember."

Mother didn't say anything. It took her some time to accept the name, for it was not really too appropriate; even now I am not nearly as big as a moose. But I am the largest mouse in the district. If it weren't for my refined features, I might often be mistaken for a rat.

I was born and brought up in a machine shop. In some respects, such as dirt and noise, it was far from an ideal home. But Mother and Father had hurriedly selected it on account of a food situation. The house they had been living in had suddenly been changed into a drugstore, and the drugstore leftovers tasted terrible.

The people who came to the machine shop every day brought with them enormous boxes of good things to eat. Every noon they would stop working and sit down to eat. And always they would carelessly drop large pieces of bread and meat and cake and fruit on the floor. And just as regularly, when they went home, all the mouse folk in the building would hurry to the floor and have a feast.

I had been taught to believe that people do not reason as we do, and that whatever they do is just from long habit, possibly a foolish habit. I was told, for instance, that whenever they find

some food, instead of eating it immediately, they often hoard it. And when they do eat it, they use tools to help them: a knife to bite the food to pieces, and still more nonsensical, two kinds of tools to push it into their mouths.

This fact seemed so ridiculous that I couldn't believe it. So I purposely watched the shop people when they ate. They didn't use any silly tools. They held their food in their front paws, mouse fashion—that is, when the food serving was the proper size.

My studies convinced me that people do reason. Creatures that can provide themselves with so much and such good food certainly are not stupid. I resolved to learn how they got it. I was ambitious to become a rich mouse with a storeroom full of food, enough to share with all the poor mice in the country.

Because I was so ambitious, I often would stay up late in the morning and creep quietly out on one of the rafters where I could watch the men at work.

I was astonished to see how well they used

their clumsy front paws. With these, they could lift great pieces of wood and iron and pass them through one of the many machines in the place. A minute later the object would come out in the form of another machine or a piece of furniture. At first I thought these were little machines being born, and that they could grow up into big ones. I learned later that this was not so and that they would never be any larger.

I admired people even more when I realized for the first time that they were not so very different from us mice. Their faces were different. They were flat and lacked our noble character. But in a way people reminded me of gigantic mice who had learned to walk on their hind legs, so they could carry things not only in their mouths but in their front paws as well. This custom struck me as very ingenious, especially when I recalled how many trips my poor mother had to make to bring a little food or bedding into our house.

I resolved that I would learn to walk on my hind legs and use my front paws as people do.

Then I would be the most efficient mouse in the world. I could already stand upright, and often did so to reach things above my head. The only problem was to keep my balance, and this skill I soon learned by walking along the wall and steadying myself with one paw. At first my leg muscles ached, but by the time the pain went away I was able to walk without even touching the wall.

I was then ready to develop my front paws. To do this I grasped a matchstick and held it high above my head. Then I would let go with either paw and swing the stick about in different directions. Soon I was adept in handling the matchstick as a cane or brandishing it like a weapon. Day after day I kept up my exercises until I felt almost as much at home on my hind legs with a stick in my paws as I did on all fours. But being sensitive and afraid of ridicule, I resolved never to show my unusual ability until some crisis made it necessary.

2

Although I was ambitious and studious and in some ways very grown up, I was nevertheless young in heart and liked fun as much as any of my young mouseling friends. The shop was a wonderful place to play, especially such games as "Run, Mousie, Run," "Hide and Seek," "Hide the Cheese," and just plain "Tag" around the big machines. The only drawback was that Mother was always complaining of my grimy paws and the greasy dirt I brought into the house.

Often we would stay up late in the morning for a particularly exciting game that we could play only after the machines were running. We never dared tell our parents about it. We called it skiing.

All over the upper part of the building there were long leather belts that moved rapidly around and ran the machines on the floor below us. The game was to jump on a belt at one end and ride swiftly to the other end. The skill and thrill was to jump off at just the right instant, before the belt disappeared around the pulley. Then we would race back along a rafter and jump on again. Delightful as the game was, it was the cause of our family's moving from the machine shop.

One morning we were skiing a little later than usual, and my mother, worrying, sent my father to call me to supper. My father's arrival at this time was, of course, an unwelcome surprise.

But as it turned out, our new sport fascinated him so much that he forgot all about his errand. Finally, he could stand it no longer. Before we experienced mouselings could caution him, he decided to try the game himself.

My heart thumped as I saw him leap on the belt, for instead of coming down on all fours as we did, he landed on his side and rolled over and over, helplessly. He struggled to his feet, but too late, and in another instant he was shot off the belt into mid air.

I stared in horror as down, down he went. It seemed many minutes that he was falling, but it was not to be as far as I had feared. For, fortunately, right below him, saving him from certain death, was a shelf. But, not so fortunately, on it was a can of oozy, smelly black cup grease. Down into the sticky grease went Father. Up he bobbed, squeaking and struggling; his paws frantically wiping the smelly stuff from his eyes and nose, and kicking all the while to keep from sinking. Never before was a dignified mouse in such a miserable mess.

Scared as we were, we mouselings rushed forward and almost tumbled to the shelf. We could see that Father's struggles couldn't long keep him from sinking out of sight. For the first time I used my great size and strength. Beside the bucket was an enormous lead pencil. Calling the other mouselings for help, I seized the pencil and raised it high above my head. Then, all together, we pushed it over the side of the can and within Father's reach.

It was hard for me to realize that the greasy, messy little object that was clinging to the pencil with his teeth and struggling over the side of the bucket was the Father who to me always seemed so upstanding and dignified. And I shall always be grateful to my playmates not only for

their help but also for not laughing at Father, as we rolled him in the sawdust to dry. And especially later, as he tried to gain his feet and skidded about as if he was intoxicated.

Naturally, in the excitement, we all lost track of time. And just as naturally, Mother, who had sent Father to bring me home, wondered what had happened. She decided to come and find out. I shall never forget her expression as she finally realized that the object that was leaving an oozy, greasy trail on the shelf, as we half-carried, half-pushed him along, was her husband.

But only for a minute was Mother speechless. "A fine mess for a grown mouse. I always expected a certain amount of dirt and grease from Moose, but thank goodness he never tried to swim in it."

Father was too humiliated to answer, and Mother's pity soon overcame her anger. She joined the rest of us in rolling him on the dry boards, and when finally we got enough of the grease out of his fur so that we could lick him, she too went to work with a will. She had always been rather proud of Father's sleek coat of charcoal grey. But like the rest of us, every time she stopped to wipe her tongue on a board, she made a face. "This stuff tastes horrible," she would say. "Why couldn't you have chosen some butter or jam to dive into?"

Finally, when the three of us reached our apartment and Mother had spread bits of paper on the floor for Father to lie on, she spoke her mind.

"This settles it. I never really liked this place, anyway, with its dirt and clatter. It's no home to bring up one mouseling, let alone two."

Father winced, but he was in no mood for argument, so she continued:

"Tomorrow, Mose, you and I will go house hunting—that is, if you smell good enough by that time."

3

I had been greatly disappointed by my mother's words and the thought of leaving my playmates, to say nothing of my studies of the shop people.

But when I saw the house that my parents selected, I felt better. It was a one-family dwelling in an exclusive part of town. As Mother said: "it had atmosphere." The house was not only the biggest one in the district, it was also the oldest. This—as every mouse householder knows—made it the best place to live in. An old dwelling has usually settled properly on its foundation, leaving plenty of headroom beneath the doors, so a mouse can go quickly

from room to room. Usually, too, there are openings in the woodwork and cracks in the plaster that make convenient short cuts.

In a world infested with cats and people, it is often most important to be able to leave a room promptly. Mice that live in new houses with tight walls, and even metal closets, often have to go out of doors just to get from room to room, and frequently have very nasty experiences.

Mother told me she once knew a family that

always had to go out of the house and under the front steps just to get into the pantry that was actually right next to their own apartment. Such a house, my mother said, wasn't fit for a decent mouse to live in.

The only bad thing about our home was that soon after we took it a family of people moved in upstairs. I complained to Father, reminding him that people are more active and make most noise in the daytime, when a growing mouse should be getting his sleep.

Father tried to comfort me. "For some reason or other, people always want to live in a house that mice are occupying, and there is very little we can do about it. Anyway, our motto should be 'Live and let live.' Also, there is another side to the picture. People are supposed to bring good luck. They say that whenever people move into a house, food seems to follow them."

Then Father told me about a family of poor mice who had to live in a church. There were no people in the building, and the whole mouse family had to hunt their food out of doors in all kinds of weather. Often the mouselings went to bed hungry. After this I felt better about letting the people live in our house.

A few days later, when they had settled down and all the noise and fuss was over, Father said: "Come, Mother, let's check up our property and see if our tenants have damaged it in any way. That will tell us what kind of folks we have to deal with."

Hardly had we got to the bottom of the stairs than Father raised his head and gave a significant sniff. "I smell cheese," he said. "That's a very good omen. What did I tell you, Moose, about people bringing good luck? We mustn't judge anyone too soon."

And sure enough, there right in front of us, resting on a neat, clean little board, was a fragrant, golden piece of cheese. We were thrilled. Father approached the board in wonder. "It's apparently an apparatus to hold the cheese and keep it from getting dirty," he said, pointing to the piece of wire that held the cheese to the board. "It's a very good idea. It's sanitary."

Mother was quite moved. "How thoughtful," she said. "I'm surprised they even knew of our presence in such a short time. They must be very considerate people."

As is the custom in the mouse family, the father should be the first to try any new food, "although," he said, "I'm sure that such generous people would serve excellent cheese."

In our wildest guess none of us could have foretold how nearly tragic was that first taste. Hardly had Father's nose sniffed the cheese, than a wire spring beneath him suddenly broke loose and tossed Father up in the air and against the wall so forcibly that he was stunned.

Mother and I were aghast and speechless. Not until Father regained consciousness did we realize how fortunate we had really been. For when we examined the cheese holder, we could see that had Father approached the cheese from the other end, instead of tossing him in

VICTORY

the air, the spring would have clamped down upon him and injured him seriously, if not fatally.

However, the force of the accident had flung the cheese loose and far across the basement, and as soon as we recovered from the nervous shock, we all actually enjoyed it despite our terrifying experience. Nevertheless, Father was so fearful that he forbade us even to go near the cheese holder again. "It's obviously defective," he said, "and the risk is too great for all the cheese in the world."

4

Father's unhappy experience brought a great change in my life. As a young mouse I had been taught it was sinful to allow good cheese to dry up and go to waste when there were so many hungry mouths in the world. Day after day my early training reproached me as I passed the holder, now containing an even more generous serving of the staff of life.

I began to question my father's judgment. Perhaps it was not very generous of me, but ever since I saved Father's life from drowning, I felt almost as if I were the older mouse, and that sooner or later I would have to be the mouse of the family. Also, modest as I was, because of my special knowledge of mechanics I knew I was much better qualified to deal with problems like a defective cheese holder. I was sure that I could repair the one in our basement.

However, I remembered Father's warning words, and I wisely refrained from touching it. Instead, I studied it thoroughly from a distance, and I had no difficulty in discovering the defect. The piece of wire that passed

through the cheese held it in place by a very carelessly made hook. Therefore the slightest touch was bound to loosen a spring beneath the hook with the terrific force that we had encountered. It was the shock of this force, too, that loosened the cheese for our benefit.

So sure was I of my facts that I brought Father and Mother to the scene and explained it to them. Mother, of course, was so nervous that she could hardly follow my words, but Father listened intently, stroking his whiskers, as was his custom when in deep thought.

At last he said seriously, "You may be right, Moose. But what can we do about it? I don't want to touch the thing again."

"We don't need to," I said excitedly, confident of my observation of mechanics. For I remembered people would use sticks or rods when they dealt with something that was either hot or too dangerous to handle.

Very self-conscious, I strode over to the woodpile in the corner and selected a stout club, larger even than a matchstick. Holding it

firmly and dramatically, I pressed it forcibly against the cheese.

"Wham!" went the spring and "squeak" went Mother. But high in the air zinged the cheese, far and safely away from the holder.

"I told you so," I said as calmly as I could under the circumstances, although Mother exclaimed, "Are we all safe?"

"We are indeed," said Father, as we all clustered about the large golden banquet. Finally, however, he got back to the subject. "How on earth did you learn so much about mechanics?"

"It's quite simple," I said. "I watched the people in the shop and saw how they did things. In some ways they are really more clever than we supposed."

"I must admit that the way you handled the situation was not very mouselike," said Father, "but it was certainly wonderful. I have no doubt your discovery will go down in history."

5

Until now, I never knew just why my mother had been so nervous about the cheese holders. Although she was vague about details, I learned that her grandfather had disappeared very mysteriously one day, just after he left his family saying that he was going down "to get some cheese." For that reason, after father's experience, she naturally concluded that her grandfather had run into some badly made appliance, just as we had. The thought that such a peril no longer existed had given her enormous relief.

She had always been a believer in green

vegetables for growing mice, but she knew the value of a protein, and the assurance of a regular supply of cheese meant a lot to her.

It was soon apparent that the people in our house didn't realize how small our family was, for a few days later there were two more cheese holders placed even more conveniently for us, just at the entrance of our apartment. Altogether, it was more cheese than we could possibly need. Whether these holders were also defective we never knew, for experience told us that the slightest touch with a matchstick would send the cheese almost into our very mouths. Even my mother, timid as she was, soon learned to help herself.

We were of course very grateful to our tenants upstairs who were so generous, and we knew that such well-meaning people would be very much upset if they knew how they had endangered our lives. But we had no way of telling them. We never met them, for they were always going to bed when we were having breakfast. Besides, the rumbling noises they made, which Father said was undoubtedly a kind of language, didn't make sense to us.

Our life was now so happy and comfortable that Mother began to think of our friends. "There's no telling," she said, "how many defective holders there may be, killing or injuring mouse folk all over the land. For all we know, maybe Mrs. Greyhouse mouse next door may be worrying, just as I used to, especially with her five young mouselings. Really, Father, I think we should let Moose run over and teach them how to operate the holders."

At Mother's words, Father's ears stood upright as they always did when he was interested. "I think you are right," he said, after a little deliberation. "Anyone as resourceful as Moose would be perfectly safe and, as you say, he might save many lives."

I could see that Father was very proud of me and that made me proud of myself. I was eager to show our friends my skill and knowledge.

So immediately after breakfast the follow-

ing evening, I started cautiously along the picket fence and across the yard between the houses. I stopped every so often to sniff the air and listen for strange sounds. The Greyhouse mice had visited us several times but we had never called on them, so I had to explore the grounds before I could find their front door—a small hole in the wall just below the porch.

Mrs. Greyhouse greeted me: "How do you do, Moose?" she said heartily. "You've grown so, I would hardly recognize you."

Although I was rather tired of being told

"how you have grown," I was nevertheless pleased that she remembered me. I was afraid I would have to introduce myself, and with so little social experience I knew my words would be very awkward. But I had come on a life and death matter, so I spoke right up.

"Mrs. Greyhouse," I said, "do you have any cheese holders in your house, and do you ever have any trouble with them?" I started to tell her of our experience, but she was so agitated I stopped short.

"Don't talk to me about them!" she exclaimed, almost as if I were to blame for something. Then she realized that I meant no offense. "You are too young to remember," she went on. "When we first moved into this house, we lost one of our mouselings because of a badly made holder. And my first husband was injured for life over the tiniest piece of cheese. In fact, there are three holders right now in our basement, and I'm only grateful that the mouselings are too young to go downstairs. But I am terrified for their future."

I could see that she was most upset, so I waited before delivering my message:

"I was afraid of that, Mrs. Greyhouse," I said. "That's why I've come over to show you and Mr. Greyhouse my discovery. I'm glad there are some holders in the basement. It's so much better to show you than to tell you about it." By this time Mr. Greyhouse had come from the rear of the house. I saw that he was a mouse of few words and that he was extremely interested in my story. "We certainly would like to know," he said thoughtfully.

"Now," I said, "if you will take me to the basement I'll show you what to do."

When I saw the holders, my confidence rose immediately. They were just like ours, and I knew I could give a perfect demonstration. Without wasting any time I went over to get a club from the woodpile.

"Stand back, please," I said, "and don't mind the noise."

Mr. Greyhouse settled back on his haunches. Mrs. Greyhouse turned her back and held her paws over her ears. I thrust the club firmly against the cheese. As I expected, "zang!" went the spring. "Wheeee," went Mrs. Greyhouse. She and her husband started to run. They were stopped by a large piece of cheese that landed right in front of them.

The Greyhouses were bewildered. They looked at the club with a puzzled expression. "It's magic," said Mrs. Greyhouse. "It certainly won't spoil the taste," said Mr. Greyhouse. I explained how simple the whole matter was as we gathered around for a banquet.

"Now, if you will take me to the other holders, I will show you how safe my method is." The next one contained so large a piece of cheese I feared it might be too heavy for the spring. So I gave a little extra thrust, with the result that the cheese flew just as high as the smaller pieces.

By this time the Greyhouses had perfect confidence in me.

"My goodness," said Mrs. Greyhouse, "this

is really wonderful! I wonder whether we could ever learn to operate the holders."

"Of course you can," I said encouragingly. "That's why I came to show you."

When we got to the third holder, I gave my club to Mr. Greyhouse. "Now," I said, "take it in your teeth and press it firmly against the cheese."

Despite his trust in me, Mr. Greyhouse approached the holder very gingerly, and his wife still averted her head. When the spring exploded, she quickly turned. There was her husband perfectly safe, while the cheese lay right before her. "It's a miracle!" she exclaimed joyously. "Now I can sleep soundly without my old nightmares."

I was extremely gratified. "If you have any further trouble," I said generously, "just send one of the mouselings and I'll be right over."

"How can we ever thank you?" she said.

"Don't mention it," I said.

6

When I returned from the Greyhouses, I told my parents not only about my success but also about our friends' former sad experience. Later, as I thought it over, I began to realize how many such cases there might be throughout the land.

"I'm young and strong," I thought to myself, "and I have plenty of time. Why shouldn't I go from house to house and show all micekind how to operate the holders?"

"But you are so young to go so far alone," said my mother when I mentioned my plan.

"Out in the world there are such things as cats and boys and dogs, and even grown people who don't like mice."

But Father thought differently. "Why not, Mother? Moose has to face the world some time. Why not now, while we are alive to advise him? We know he will be careful, especially when he remembers how many lives may depend on him. Who knows, maybe he will be another Paul Revere!"

I didn't know anything about Paul Revere at the time. I later learned that he was a famous mouse who could run extra fast, and that when Mouseland was suddenly threatened by a dangerous enemy he ran swiftly from house to house warning all mice. As a result the enemy was beaten and Mouseland was saved.

One reason I think Father liked my idea was that he felt the matter was important, and that if I didn't make the trip he should do it. He didn't like to exert himself. He was well past middle age, and Mother said that even when he was younger he would prefer to sit quietly and think things out while she got the work done.

"He was very ingenious," Mother said. "If he had had your education in mechanics and your ambition, I'm sure he would have been a very great mouse. Every time we moved into a new house he would modernize the building in a few days—a task that would take an ordinary mouse many weeks. He knew just how

to gnaw the boards properly and just where to make the holes for the necessary short cuts to the kitchen, from all directions. This saved time and steps, and maybe even our lives."

Mother's words made me proud of my father and even more proud of his confidence in me. I could see that my mother, although fearful, was greatly stirred at the thought that I might become a hero.

"I'll start tomorrow," I said, when we had discussed the matter at length. Nevertheless, I was glad to sit down with my father, who told me what to do on encounters with dogs and cats and small boys. I was especially impressed by his advice as to when it was better to run and when to remain motionless—advice I was to use many times in the future.

"People don't see as well as we do," my father said. "Often they will notice you only when you are moving. As an experiment, once I sat out in a garden all day and let people pass right by me. They didn't notice me. But the moment I moved, there was great excite-

ment. And so I came to the conclusion that sometimes when you are outnumbered it is safer to stand still than to run away."

The next morning Mother made up a little lunch for me—portions of bread and cheese and chicken wrapped up in a piece of apple peel.

"Here, Moose," she said, "you may meet a poor mouse who would appreciate a bit of chicken. Or you might get hungry yourself. But be very careful."

Father went with me as far as the fence. He pointed the way to the house where I should make my first visit. I should follow the fence line until I reached the one with the red door. He repeated some of the advice he had already given me. "Usually the best approach to any house is beneath the front or back steps. The Red Door mouse folks live in the dining room wall. Look ahead carefully before venturing out on the lawn and then cross the open space quickly.

"In journeying along fences, which is the

7

As I started on my great adventure, I found that, mouselike, I was carrying my lunch bag in my teeth. I realized this would be most inconvenient. For one thing, it prevented me from looking about as freely as I should on such a dangerous journey. Since I was able to walk upright and carry my lunch in my paw, I grasped the bag firmly and rose up on my hind legs. At first I walked cautiously along the fence. But what a thrill it was to stand upright and meet the world face to face. Surely no mouse on an important mission had ever been able to look about like this.

My mind was still full of Father's parting

FRESH
MILK

advice as I followed along the fence in back of the Grey House. When I got opposite the Red Door House, I went directly to the back steps and beneath the basement door. As I entered the basement I stopped suddenly, for my nostrils caught an overwhelming smell.

"A cat," I thought fearfully. I crouched in a corner, wondering whether to escape and move on to another, perhaps catless, house. However, hearing and seeing nothing, I soon recovered my courage. After all, lives were at stake. Cautiously I followed along the mudsill until I found the well-worn mouse path to the Red Door mouse home. Once within the apartment, I felt relieved. But after introducing myself and stating my errand, I ventured to inquire about the smell.

"Could it be, Mrs. Mousewife, that there is a cat living with you?"

"Gracious, no," she said, horror stricken. "We wouldn't stay in a house one minute with a cat about. We're not stuck up or anything, but cats are not fit acquaintances, especially when there is a family of growing little ones. The smell you noticed is garlic. We were very much disturbed when the people first brought it into the building. Father, in fact, spent an entire evening carrying it out and dumping it into the back yard. But it did no good. The people brought more of it the next day. However, as they were good tenants in other respects we decided to put up with it. Strange as it may seem now, we not only got used to it but we actually learned to enjoy it. When we have guests we sometimes serve it as a relish. And Father, who likes it most of all, insists it helps his rheumatism."

Now, being at ease, I hurried on to my business. I learned that, like many others, my hosts had had at least one bad experience with a holder, and that thereafter they avoided the contraption as too dangerous. As there was only one holder in the house, I quickly carried out the purpose of my visit.

At the next house, and the next, it was the same story. In each family there had been at least one tragic experience, and all of the oc-

cupants were delighted when I showed them how to get the cheese without any risk. One of the mothers actually shed tears. "It's so wonderful," she said, "after all these years to be able to count on a regular supply of food delivered right to our front door."

8

By this time I was tired and felt that I was entitled to a little breathing spell. The garden before me looked most inviting. I decided to take a little nap in the cool shade of the ivy that edged the lawn.

Remembering my father's counsel, I kept beneath the overhanging leaves. It was well that I did. For hardly had I gone a quarter of the way, when I saw the most terrifying object I had ever beheld. I had no need to ask questions: the huge creature before me with the cruel yellow half-closed eyes was none other than the archenemy of my race and the bugaboo of our dreams—a cat. For the moment I was so frightened that I could not have fled if I had tried.

Surely no mouse ever faced such a problem. Here I was on a life or death mission and I must go on. But before me was the most blood-thirsty of all creatures. From beneath the over-hanging leaves that hid me, I looked anxiously ahead, especially noting the long board fence to my right. As I hoped, it was riddled with mouse holes its whole length. I would stay as close to it as possible. In an emergency I would escape into the next yard.

Feeling safer, my courage came back to me, and also a feeling of indignation. The creature before me was an enemy that had preyed upon my people all through the ages. It was high time that some great mouse rose up and ended the long reign of terror. Who knows, maybe I was destined to be that hero.

Stirred by the idea, I no longer feared him. But I knew it was poor generalship to meet any enemy on his own grounds. I would avoid conflict for the present, but I would go on at all costs.

Plucking an ivy leaf large enough to conceal me, I approached the edge of the lawn I must cross. I bit a hole in the leaf and peeked through it. The enemy was now looking in the other direction. I stood up to my full height, and holding the leaf above me, I started across the lawn that might or might not be my final resting place. I kept one eye on the nearest hole in the fence and the other on the cat. Remembering Father's advice, I stopped the instant he turned his head. I was now halfway across, but I could see that he had become interested in the leaf that had suddenly appeared on the lawn. Stupid as he was, he had noticed its changing position.

Then came the moment I feared. Rising to his feet, he pointed his nose in my direction. Slowly and curiously he crept toward me. I dropped the leaf and dashed for the nearest knothole. No longer in doubt, the cat with one fierce leap covered half the distance between us. However, I was now within inches of safety, and to show my contempt for him I remained at the entrance of the hole as if waiting for him. When he was almost upon me, I calmy passed through into the next yard.

I am sure that, from a mouse viewpoint, many would have thought that I had shown great courage. Strangely enough, I didn't feel so. Indeed, I was really ashamed of the fact that I had to run. Why should I, or anyone, have to fear other creatures? The thought that such a low, sneaking character had terrified my people since the beginning of time roused my fury. Some day, when the opportunity came, I would strike a blow at all mouse preyers.

My first chance came sooner than I expected. A huge black paw was suddenly thrust through the hole just after me. Carefully avoiding the terrible claws, I bit sharply into the soft furry flesh. I know that such an act was not noble of me, but the angry yowl that followed the frantic withdrawal was music to my ears.

I was now sure of my tactics. I knew that

the cat would nose along the fence for an opening and also that there was no hole large enough for him. As I hoped, he immediately climbed the fence. But the glare he cast in my direction no longer alarmed me. The fence was very narrow, and he was awkward and uncomfortable when he paused to spring. I waited to give him hope of catching me. Then I blithely went through the fence. I heard him sniffing angrily behind me but this time there was no mouse-hunting paw reaching through for me to bite. I had taught him one lesson at least.

Hurrying to another hole a few feet away, I shook a geranium plant to get his attention. He came bounding toward me. I waited till the last moment. I repeated this maneuver several times, always being careful to use a different hole as far away as possible. Finally thoroughly disgusted, he ignored me completely. He scaled the fence and settled on the lawn to lick his bitten paw wearily.

So confident of myself was I now that I decided to experiment. Standing upright to my full height I slowly walked toward him, taking care not to get too far from the fence. Instead of turning toward me, my dreaded enemy actually looked away, blinking his eyes uneasily. I am sure that he had never before seen a mouse standing on its hind legs and coming toward him.

As I look back upon the incident I feel sure that had I suddenly rushed toward him he would have fled. But, on the other paw, he might not have. And my life at the time was far too valuable to lose to a worthless cat. Never-

theless, I felt so safe that I made a circuit of the house. Entering the basement through a porch lattice, I learned what I had already suspected—there was no mouse family living in the house.

9

After my interrupted nap and exciting adventure I was hungry. I felt now even more entitled to a breathing spell. And since I had not encountered any little hungry mouse, such as my mother mentioned, I decided I would be the hungry mouse myself. So I turned back to the lunch that I had hidden under a leaf at the first sight of the cat.

Having time to look about me, I saw that I was in a strange new land of gardens, trees, and beautiful flowers. So, momentarily carrying my lunch between my teeth, I climbed the highest of the fence posts and settled down to enjoy the scenery with my food.

For the first time I got an idea of how large the world really was, and I wondered why we mouse folk had been content to live cooped up in walls and basements when it was so pleasant outside. I resolved that once I had made the world safe for mice I would travel far and see more of it. Perhaps with my mechanical learning I could bring back new and useful knowledge.

After finishing the last bit of chicken, I wiped my lips with a small clean leaf, as my mother had always taught me to do. Then I stood up to get a better look of the road ahead of me.

The house I had just visited was the last one on the road and just beyond was a wide street with a lot of big noisy machines rushing by in both directions. I knew they were automobiles, for I had seen them many times in garages I had visited. But I had never heard their roaring at close range, and I had never thought of crossing the street in front of them.

I continued the short remaining journey

along the top of the fence. When I reached the end and looked down, I confess I felt much less like going out into the world.

The idea of being crushed beneath those tremendous wheels did not appeal to me, and I even thought of turning back.

But then the thought of the mouse folk who might be in peril this very minute strengthened my spirit. Across the street on the corner was the grocery store. Mother and Father had often spoken of the Grocery Mice, sometimes I thought with a little envy. The Grocery Mice were the wealthiest we knew. Not that they put on any airs, but all during the cold weather and hard times they had never felt the pinch of poverty like the rest of us.

While these thoughts were passing through my head, it was growing dark. I knew there would be fewer people on the street and also fewer automobiles. I slipped down the fence post and ran over to the curb. Once there, I hurried along the gutter to the corner.

On the opposite side was the grocery store.

For a long time I waited to get up my courage to dash between the thundering automobiles. Then something unexpected and wonderful happened, and I didn't know how I accomplished it.

The moment I started across the street I heard a loud whistle, and suddenly all the cars stopped to let me cross in front of them. Not wishing to detain such considerate drivers any longer than necessary, I hurried across. The moment I touched the curb, the whistle shrilled again and the automobiles started once more.

The incident gave me a feeling of importance and self-assurance, although I realized that many things that seem like miracles often have simple explanations. With spirit, I related my experience to the Grocery Mice as soon as the first greeting was over.

"We've come to the conclusion that it's the whistle that does it," said Mr. Grocery Mouse.

"Oh," I said rather hopefully. "Then after this in my travels I will bring a whistle with me." Mr. Grocery Mouse looked dubious. "I think it would have to be a very loud one. But, to tell the truth, I have never thought much about it, for we seldom have to cross the street. We have everything we will ever need right here in our house. The only time we cross streets is when we go visiting."

He was certainly right about having everything they could possibly need within reach. I entered their house beneath a big door. There I found myself in the midst of a fabulous situation—an enormous room, stacked high on all sides with every imaginable kind of food.

It was supper time and the clan were at various stages of dining. They were scattered all around the big room, wherever the food happened to be to their taste. Some of the late comers were still mincing at their green vegetables, bits of lettuce, cabbage and nibbles of carrot. Others were feasting on the helpings of boiled ham, sausage and bacon that were beneath the huge slicing machine.

Mrs. Grocery Mouse was enjoying a large luscious prune that she had dragged out of a box onto the floor. She moved over in a friendly way. "Try it," she said to me. "The prunes are especially good this season."

Although I started to partake of their food for politeness' sake, I helped to finish the prune because it was so delicious.

"I thank you very sincerely, Mrs. Grocery Mouse," I said, "but I have really come on a serious matter. All the mouse folk I have visited have had terrible experiences with their cheese holders."

Mrs. Grocery Mouse was plainly surprised, but she listened carefully as I told my story. When I finished, she said: "I can truthfully say that we never had any trouble with our cheese holder. But I judge it is very different from the ones you describe. Although ours is large, it is very simple." With that, she led me up to the first shelf. Before my eyes, on a large round board, was a huge mountain of cheese beneath an enormous glass cover. Never had I dreamt that there could be so much cheese in any one place, and at first I could only stare in wonder.

"As you see," she said, "there is a cover over it, and at first we would depend only on the crumbs from the cuttings that were scattered around on the outside. But Percy, our oldest mouseling—who, if I do say it myself, is very bright—showed us that if we all got together and pushed the cover over the edge of the board we could then climb up onto the cheese board.

When we finished, we always pushed the cover back to keep the cheese nice and fresh."

In one way my visit to the store mice was rather discouraging. They didn't need my help. But it was encouraging to know that mice could have such a high standard of living. It could be an inspiration to us all.

Nevertheless, all I could say as I left was, "it's nice you have such enlightened and generous tenants living with you. But why do they store up so much food just for you two families?"

"Oh, I'm sure they share their food with people. We hear strangers coming and going all day long, and we are positive they take quantities of food away with them. For often, when we go down for breakfast, we find that certain delicacies we couldn't finish the night before are missing. But as long as someone else is able to enjoy them we don't resent it."

As I journeyed on, I was soon able to reassure myself as to the good I was doing. Family after family had suffered in some way from cheese holders. Many mice had broken legs or had tails cut off by the sharp spring. Those that survived were very bitter and warned everybody to avoid cheese at all costs. Because of this, many of those I met looked pinched and undernourished.

But the most poverty-stricken family I saw were the Church Mouse family Father had told me about. They had had no accidents because they had had no cheese holders and very little food.

"It is true, as your father told you," said Mrs. Church Mouse, "church people seldom eat more than once a month. Of course, when they do, there is a lot left over. But it doesn't last forever with six mouths to feed. All the rest of the month we have to depend upon what Father and I can bring in from hunting trips. Father is a good hunter, but personally I am getting tired of wild game like grasshoppers, crickets and cockroaches. I'd love to get my teeth into a piece of Swiss cheese, or cold chicken, or roast beef like I used to get when I was young."

While she was talking, I couldn't help thinking of Mrs. Greyhouse, who complained that she so seldom got any wild game.

"In spite of what you say," Mrs. Church Mouse went on, "I almost wish someone would bring us a nice big holder full of cheese, especially since you tell me they can be used safely. But, anyway, you can be sure that just as soon as we find a suitable house, we'll move. And this time we'll make sure we have tenants who eat every day."

"I certainly wish you luck," I said warmly, "and when you do move, call me before you use the holders."

10

I had been looking forward to my visit to the School Mouse family. Their building was across the street from the toffee shop. And by the way, I found the toffee shop mouselings were not nearly so happy as other mouselings would expect. Mrs. Toffee Mouse explained that her children ate far too many sweets, and that she had a hard time getting them to eat wholesome bread, meat and salads. Usually at mealtime they had very little appetite.

Although I, myself, was very fond of sweets, I was mature enough to see the wisdom of her complaints. And I said sagely, "it is possible to have too much of a good thing."

"Young as you are," she replied, "I can see that you are very wise."

I was soon to see the beneficial results of sensible living when I arrived across the street where the School Mice lived. They were a large group of many related families. They had dwelt for generations in an immense building and had grown up together. They were a healthy, happy lot; not as stout as the Grocery Mice, perhaps because they had more room for play and exercise.

Naturally a well-informed group, the School Mice were very much interested in my crusade as I recounted my adventures and successes on behalf of mouse folk.

"It is a very noble venture," said Father Schoolmouse, when I had finished. "We, ourselves, are not in any peril. We do have cheese holders in the basement, but they are very poorly serviced and we just ignore them. The stingy little pieces of cheese in them are many days old. They don't compare with our other sources of food."

As if to convince me, Mrs. Schoolmouse, rather proudly I thought, led me through room after room, showing me large wire baskets which, she said, during the day contained innumerable portions of school lunches—such things as ham and tongue and sardines, bits of apple, banana, bread, butter and cake.

"We don't even have to come after it," she explained. "The caretaker—he's the person we have to take care of our building for us—gathers up the baskets and empties them down in our dining quarters. He is very prompt and regular and always has it there in time for our evening breakfast. For that meal we gather from all quarters of the building. It is really a banquet every evening."

Never had I met a family who were so carefree. Much of the day and all of the night they had the building to themselves.

"One of the best things about our building," one mother told me, "is that we have a playroom for each different age group of mouselings. There is practically no squabbling and no interference from oldsters. There is even more play equipment than we really need. Each mouse, if he wants to, can have his own private ruler for a slide, or a pencil to roll. Never since we moved here have I been bothered by the old cry, 'What is there to do?' "

Interesting as my whole visit with the School Mice was, nothing gave me a thrill like my meeting with the venerable Mr. Wisemouse. Wisemouse was a famous philosopher. He had made a lifelong study of people. It was he who later proved through a series of tests that people reasoned just as mice do, and that the loud rumbling from their throats was a kind of language. And, further, he discovered they could talk to each other without any noise, by making funny little scratches on the blackboard and on paper. But his outstanding accomplishment was that he had learned and understood their blackboard language.

Nevertheless, he was so modest that when I met him I was immediately at ease. And I was elated to know that he had already heard of my work.

"Moose," he said, "you are really doing wonderful educational work. It will save thousands of lives. I've been told that you are a self-made mouse, and that your understanding of machinery is due entirely to your own studies. I know very little about mechanics and engineering, and I am sure there are many things you could teach me."

He was so encouraging that before long I was telling him all about my life in the machine shop, and what I had learned about people and their ability to do many things just because they could use their front paws so cleverly. And when I timidly mentioned to him my theory that originally people were large mouselike creatures that had learned to walk on their hind legs and so have their paws free to work with, he became quite excited.

"Moose," he exclaimed, "you really are a born scientist. I have lived many more years than you have, yet your simple theory never occurred to me. I am sure you are right, and that if we would train ourselves to use our front paws we, too, could build ourselves big houses and machines to ride in. Nor would we have to live from paw to mouth each day, as so many mice do at present."

There was no doubt that Wisemouse was truly impressed with my ideas, but I was even more interested to hear how he learned people's language.

"It was much easier than one would expect," he said, "especially for one dwelling in a school.

You see," he went on, "unlike little mice that are born blind, little people instead are born speechless. They not only can't talk, they can't even understand talk. They have to go to school to learn their own language. But what's funnier," Wisemouse went on, "people have many different languages and the majority of them can't understand each other." This seemed so absurd that we both laughed out loud. "So all I had to do was just to go to school with the little people. I didn't use a desk. My presence would have terrified them. I found a comfortable place in the balcony and memorized the lessons with them.

"I must say that their method of teaching is very clever. First they show an object or a picture of an object. Then, at the same time, they make a special noise and draw funny little signs. All three mean the same thing. For instance, they showed a picture of a cat, and made the noise that meant 'cat' and drew the letters that spell a cat. All I had to do was to look and listen.

CAT

"Because of my mature mind and because my sight and hearing are so much keener than theirs, it was much easier for me than for the little people. So I was able to move along from class to class much faster than they could. 'Skipping grades,' they call it."

As he went on, however, Wisemouse seemed sad. "But in a way my success is disappointing. For instance, there is no doubt that the cheese holders are faulty. But I can't tell people about it! Their ears are far too dull to hear my voice. I have even called out to them at the top of my lungs, and they don't seem to hear me ."

As I listened to Wisemouse, his achievement seemed very great. The fact that a mouse could learn people's language in less time than a person could was a great tribute to my race. At the same time I, too, felt how disappointing it all was.

Nevertheless, I was stimulated and elated, especially by Wisemouse's parting words.

"Moose," he said in front of the assembled mouse folk, "we don't for one moment belittle your great work just because we don't happen to need your knowledge at present. I have lived long enough to know there will always be new problems in the mouse world, and at any moment we may need your skill and wisdom. I know that all of the mouse folk here tonight thank you, in the name of the underprivileged mice whose lives you have saved."

As I went home I realized that I had been so interested that it never occurred to me to tell Wisemouse of my own skill with my front paws. I am sure it would have encouraged him. More than ever, now, I would devote myself to my weight-lifting and finger exercises.

11

The days that followed my crusade were probably the happiest that Mouseland had ever known. Mothers no longer feared to let their children play in basements. The first thing parents did each evening was to release the cheese in the holders. The bang no longer terrified anyone. It was now a welcome sound.

I was very happy about the whole affair. I had become a hero. I was very much gratified by the praise of the mouse mothers when they called on my mother. I was constantly hearing such words as, "I haven't slept so well for years. We just can't thank Moose enough. You should be proud of him."

As I look back, now I realize that we mouse folk should not have expected such a happy period to last. For history shows that our lives have always been beset with risk and danger. As it was, just when we were feeling most secure, one night we had a very disturbing visitor. I recognized him immediately. It was Henry Schoolmouse, the oldest of the school mouselings. He was breathless and excited.

"Uncle Wisemouse sent me and I ran all the way," he said. "He wanted me to tell Moose because he knows all the mousefolk."

"What's it all about?" I asked, almost as excited as he was.

Henry paused for breath. "You know, in the place where we live, people often hold meetings at night when the young ones have left. They probably talk about things they don't want their children to hear. Each time they put up a sign telling what the next meeting is for. Uncle Wisemouse, as you know, understands people's language. This morning the people were very much excited when they gathered around the blackboard, and when he got there he was excited too. The sign said, 'The Growing Mouse Problem.' "

I don't know whether it was Henry's tone or not, but we were all dismayed by his words. It was, of course, the first time any of us had ever heard a direct message from people. And the first message was a disturbing one. Father was silent for a long time. "It may be very serious," he said.

Being less experienced, I was more hopeful. "Perhaps it just means that they are running out of cheese and will have to cut down on our helpings."

"Perhaps," said Father absently. But he didn't sound convinced. "Anyway," he said, "don't say anything to your mother. You know how nervous she is."

We had forgotten Henry, for the moment, until he spoke again. "Anyway," he said, "Uncle Wisemouse says all of the mouse people should attend the meeting too. And that Moose should tell everyone to come. Uncle Wisemouse will explain what the people are saying about us."

In spite of the seriousness of the situation, I could see that Father was very proud of the expressed confidence in his son.

"You are indeed another Paul Revere," he said, again bringing up the funny name.

Long before the meeting, the mouse folk had gathered beneath the schoolhouse steps. I had told them all to go separately instead of marching in a body. "It is important that we are not seen," I said, "for people are afraid of us, and we might break up the meeting." When we had all assembled, Mr. Schoolmouse led us up the back stairs to the balcony of the big room. It was comfortably dark in the spot he had prepared for us. We could not be seen, yet we could see and hear everything.

While we were waiting for the meeting to begin, Mr. Wisemouse told us about former meetings he had attended.

"Usually," he said, "the meetings are about

their children. It seems that young people are not as well-behaved as young mice. They often don't learn what they are told. They quarrel or they eat too much and get sick. Indeed, they have problems we never have."

While Uncle Wisemouse was talking, the hall had filled up. And, just as I was getting impatient, a man person suddenly rose up in front of the others. He pounded on the table with a funny piece of wood, although he didn't seem angry.

"Ladies and gentlemen," he said. Wisemouse explained his words as he spoke. "This meeting is very important. We have a problem that is not only new but unheard of. For generations mice have been a nuisance to us, and we have set traps for them and always have caught a great many. For the past two weeks we have set our traps. But they now take the cheese and we haven't caught a single mouse. Everyone in this room tonight has complained that he has set his traps as usual, only to lose the cheese."

While the man was speaking, and before we knew what he was saying, we saw the horror-stricken look on Wisemouse's face.

"So that's what the cheese holders are," he exclaimed. "They are not defective. They are traps to kill us." We were all aghast. Some mice screamed. It was a shock to learn that we were living with creatures that had always wanted to destroy us. Instead of sharing their cheese with us, they were luring us to our death.

Wisemouse recovered enough to speak: "Mouse folk, I know how you all feel. It's unthinkable to remain in the presence of the creatures that want to kill you. But we must listen to the rest of the meeting and learn what to expect." Several mouse folk started to speak.

"Shhh," said Wisemouse. "They're all excited."

"Our traps are useless," said the speaker. "Some very clever mouse has learned how to spring them and get the cheese."

Although shocked, I was nevertheless flattered as the man went on:

"The problem is a serious one because we are dealing with an enemy that we seldom see. In the past, traps have been our best attack. We have hired cats, but they are unreliable. If we don't feed them, they won't stay; and if we do, they get fat and lazy and won't catch mice."

There was now so much discussion that even Wisemouse couldn't understand it all. He did learn, however, that the man felt the whole question was too serious to be settled in one meeting, and he had appointed a committee to plan ways of getting rid of us mice. The committee would report the following week.

12

You can imagine how disturbed and excited we all were after the meeting. The people had left and we were alone in the big room where we had heard such terrible news. Now, for the first time, I could look about and see who was present. It was undoubtedly the largest and most varied gathering of mouse folk ever assembled. Even our distant relatives from the woods and fields had rallied to our call. My reflections were cut short by the voice of Wisemouse, who, although the smallest mouse in the room, was recognized as our leading spirit.

"Mouse folk," he said in an agitated voice, "this is indeed a tragic situation. That another

kind of creature wants to destroy us is a terrible thought. But we mustn't lose courage. Although people are many times larger than we are, and have been trying to exterminate us for centuries, they have been unsuccessful. This is a tribute to our intelligence and our enduring qualities. But the time is here now to decide how we are to treat people in the future. I hope you will all express your minds freely."

Even before Wisemouse had finished, Butcher Shop Mouse was on his feet.

"We have no choice," he said. "We must fight. We can't stand idly by and be destroyed. We have a right to live. People are naturally cowards. That's why they have to resort to traps. They dare not fight us, man to mouse without weapons, as we would do. I repeat, we must fight."

There was much applause when Butcher Mouse sat down. But the next moment Father Fieldmouse raised his paw to get attention.

Wisemouse recognized him immediately. "Mr. Fieldmouse, you have something to say?"

"I should say I have," rejoined Fieldmouse. "I partially agree with Brother Butcher Mouse. I claim that people are not only cowards but ungrateful cowards. As you all know, my kinfolk are a hardy race. We have always been frontiersmice. We never bent the knee to people as some folks have had to do. We have never sought the shelter of their houses. We have foraged for our own food. And not only for our benefit alone. We have protected people from all kinds of destructive creatures. We have consumed millions of weed seeds that would have destroyed their crops.

"Even men must acknowledge our heroic part in the historic crisis of the western plains, when grasshopper hordes descended on the farms and threatened to destroy everything. While people were in their churches praying for deliverance, we met the enemy head on. We finally vanquished them, although we must give full credit to the sea gulls from the big lake and other courageous birds who joined us."

Fieldmouse stopped a moment for breath.

"It is true," he went on, "we did eat some of the food we salvaged. But I ask you: who deserved it as much as we did?

"And as for the common charge that mice bring germs into the houses: that is nonsense. Personally, I don't think there are such things as germs: I have never seen one; I doubt that any of you have, either." While Fieldmouse was speaking, paws were raised and many called out, "What is a germ?"

At this point, Wisemouse had to explain.

"According to people's belief, a germ is a very, very small creature that gets into people's food and into the air they breathe, and often results in poison and death. According to this belief, germs are not only too small for people to see but even too small for a mouse to see."

At this point the audience burst into laughter. Fieldmouse interrupted. "The idea that anything too small for a mouse to see can kill a creature as big as a person is all poppycock."

There was a long pause after Fieldmouse's speech. We were greatly moved. Many of us had never before heard about the heroic deeds of our race. However, the great moment of our meeting was yet to come.

Suddenly there was a stirring in the back of the room. I looked around. The crowd quietly parted, and there appeared the most startling, yet beautiful, vision that I had ever seen: a pure white mouse with beautiful pink eyes and pink-lined ears. Modestly, but determinedly, she approached the speaker's platform.

As Miss Whitemouse passed near me on her way to the platform, I had a queer feeling, and for a good reason. When I was very young and my mother wished to get me to sleep, she would often tell me bedtime stories. Some of them would be true, great adventures of famous mice; others, fanciful tales about big buildings made entirely of cheese, and about apples so large that a mouse family could eat their way into the core and live there for years.

But of all the stories, the one I remembered most clearly was her telling me that when mice died they went to another world, and there they became what she called "angels." Angel mice were always pure white, and they lived forever in a land where there were no people and no cats and no other unfriendly creatures. As I had always cherished this story best of all, suddenly to come face to face with an apparent angel was very exciting.

There was a hush as Miss Whitemouse mounted the chalk box that served as a speaker's platform. For such a delicate creature, her voice was clear and earnest.

"I know," she said, "that my presence here is very unexpected, but when I heard about the attack on my race, I felt I must come and speak to you.

"First of all I want to correct the common impression most mouse people have about the white mouse family. It is thought that because so many of us live in hospitals and laboratories and stores that we are a sickly race or lack courage. It is true that most of us do live in such places, but not because we want to." Her voice rose with great emotion. "We are there as pris-

oners! Ages and ages ago many white mice were made captive. Since that time we have lived and grown up in wire prisons—'cages' people politely call them. We are well-fed and housed and secure—but what is that to liberty?"

The audience was spellbound as she went on:

"Fortunately my immediate family escaped several generations ago. Otherwise I wouldn't be with you tonight. But we keep in touch with our relatives. We visit them secretly. They keep us informed about people. That is how I have the knowledge I bring.

"Difficult as it may be to believe, there are such things as germs, as we now know to our sorrow. They are the cause of our misery. People use us to test germs for their own safety. If mice are healthy, they poison them with dangerous germs to make them ill; then they give them other germs to learn how to make them well again. We know they do this for a very good purpose for themselves, but not for us. They want to learn what germs keep *them* well.

"For the knowledge they get they take all the credit and boast of all the lives they save. But they never mention how many mouse lives have been sacrificed to do it." Miss Whitemouse's voice choked up as she went on. "And now they are doing the most despicable thing of all: they blame us for germs.

"How unfair they are! I don't want to say anything against our fellow creatures, the birds. But very few birds have served people as we have. Yet people build special houses for them. They have feeders for them. They have fountains for them. If, as they complain, people don't want us in their houses, why do they leave entrances for us, making us believe we are welcome? They don't do that for mosquitoes or even for birds. What a pity it is we can't present our case at their meeting."

After a moment to gain her composure, Miss Whitemouse got down from the rostrum and went to her seat amid a tumult of squeaks of applause and indignation.

Of all those carried away by her eloquence, the most moved was Wisemouse.

"Friends," he said, "like you I have just listened to what is perhaps the greatest speech in mouse history. Yet I have to confess it brings me nothing but sadness; for in this bitter moment I realize that all my so-called wisdom counts for nothing. I have learned the language of people, but I can't speak to them. I can't write to them. I have paid so little attention to my physical condition that I can't even hold a piece of chalk or pencil in my paws, much less write with it."

At the very first, I had been stirred by Butcher Mouse's courageous call to arms. But as I listened to calmer words, I realized that even victory would not bring peace. If we won a war, the people who were left would always hate us and would still try to kill us. We would never feel comfortable. Wisemouse finished on a note of such sadness that I felt a sob rising in my throat. But the next instant my spirits rose excitedly. I could hold chalk in my paws! With his guidance I could write to people!

Although bashful in crowds I suddenly leaped to the platform. "Mr. Wisemouse," I exclaimed. "There is something I must tell you! I can use my front paws just as people do. I am sure I can write words if you will guide me."

There was a general hush throughout the room. I could see the older mouse folk were annoyed, thinking I was trying to attract attention to myself at a tragic moment. Stung to action, I ran quickly to the side wall and clambered up the wainscoting onto the wooden ledge at the bottom of the blackboard. I seized a piece of chalk in my two front paws. Holding it firmly I walked along the ledge on my hind legs, dragging out a long straight line. Then I swung the chalk back and forth and made funny little figures, two of which by chance happened to be people's letters. Below, the mouse folk looked on dumbfounded.

Even Wisemouse seemed stunned. Then in a broken voice he exclaimed: "At last! At Last!" Although he didn't say at last what.

The whole room was squeaking with excitement when I dropped to the floor. Everyone crowded around me. The younger mice especially were thrilled. They felt my front paw muscles, and even imitated me as I stood erect.

Wisemouse was on the verge of tears.

"Moose," he said, "you have perhaps saved us from a long and bloody struggle. Never again will I belittle physical strength. Tell us, how did you ever build up your physique to such perfection?"

Although embarrassed by the sudden attention, I simply told of my early life in the machine shop. I repeated how I had observed the greater efficiency of people just because they could use their two front paws, saving their mouth for such few special needs as holding small tools, pencils and the like.

It was indeed a moment of triumph. As the crowd dispersed, Wisemouse took me aside.

"We must get together as soon as possible. People are no doubt even now preparing for war. We must practice together. Then we must meet here the afternoon before the people's next meeting and write our message."

I eagerly agreed. All the way home, and even when I was coiled up in my shredded paper mattress, my mind was so filled with great new ideas that I had a hard time getting to sleep.

13

It was late afternoon before the people's meeting. Wisemouse and I arrived early at the school building, waiting only for the little people to leave. Then we clambered up onto the chalk rail.

"Moose," he said, "I won't take the time now to explain the words. We have a long message to write. Later I will teach you people's language. Besides you will learn much of it as you write. Just follow me as I point."

I picked up the chalk and held it firmly in my two front paws. Standing my full height I carefully followed Wisemouse's nose across the blackboard, making firm clear marks as we

moved along. The chalk was large and hard to hold, even for my powerful paws. Frequently I had to pause to rest my muscles, and for the first time I realized the tremendous job before me. This was fortunate, for it set my mind to work.

"Wisemouse," I said, "it would be much easier and I could work faster if I made the chalk thinner and easier to hold."

Wisemouse grasped the fact quickly. "But what can we do about it?" he asked.

"It's not difficult," I said. I laid the chalk down and held my teeth firmly against it while I revolved it with my strong front paws, just as I had seen shop people do with a lathe. Wisemouse was puzzled until he saw the growing pile of chalk dust, while the chalk got thinner and thinner. Then he joined in the task at the far end. Of course, like me, he found the chalk far from tasty, and we often had to stop and wipe the dust from our noses and whiskers. But soon we had the chalk stick one half its original thickness. I could hold it firmly in one paw alone.

"How did you ever think of such an ingenious process?" he asked.

"I can't take the credit," I answered. "Shop people do things like that all the time, when they are making things. Only they have a machine to do the turning and a little iron tooth to do the biting."

As a result of my idea I could write almost as fast as Wisemouse could lead me, and we finished our work sooner than we had expected.

"Moose, you have a wonderful mind," Wisemouse said, as we came to a stopping place. "Some day you are going to be a very famous mouse."

Pausing only to go over the spelling, we both dropped to the floor and mounted a desk opposite the blackboard to see how our message would appear to the people.

"This is an historic moment," said Wisemouse. "The first words between mice and men. Little mice will be told about it in the years to come." As he spoke, he looked proudly at the blackboard. Then he said, "I'll translate it:

> "To the School People:
>
> We know now that you are trying to destroy us. But you have no right to. We have always protected you from your real enemies. We have devoured the roaches, beetles, grasshoppers, mosquitoes and other creatures that otherwise would invade your homes. When hordes of grasshoppers threatened your wheat fields, we saved them for

you. We eat weed seeds that destroy your crops.

"You say we bring germs. The truth is that thousands of our white cousins have died in your laboratories to save you from germs.

"Birds eat insects also, but they do not protect you from germs. Yet you build houses for them. You provide them with feeders. Why not mouse feeders so that we can keep our food clean?

"We don't want war. We don't want to poison your food, or kill you with germs, or set fire to your houses by gnawing the wires, or do any of the terrible things we can do if you force us to. We want peace.

"Truly yours—The School Mouse Protective Association"

I was thrilled as I heard my writing read back to me. Although thoroughly tired, nevertheless I was so inspired that I asked, "What do we do next?" Wisemouse seemed startled.

"I should think we've worked enough for

a while. We have to attend the people's meeting later. We must know immediately whether it will be war or peace. In the meantime," he continued, "we should replenish our strength, and I think a little food is in order although it is early. Let's go to the basement and take a sniff at the menu." Despite my ambitious mood, I heartily agreed with Wisemouse.

In the basement was a long line of wastebaskets that had been emptied into a large bin. From hearsay, I knew that each wastebasket had contained a generous amount of good food. In the bin, lodged in and about crumpled papers, were appetizing portions of sandwiches as large as a mouse, pieces of cake with chocolate frosting, tasty fruit, pie, fresh apples, nuts, hard-boiled eggs and meats of all kinds. While not so well served, the spread was even more varied and challenging than the grocery store menu. And as to after-dinner cheeses, Wisemouse assured me many of the varieties had been imported from foreign countries.

Never before so tempted, it was little wonder I ate far too much. Worst of all, at the point when another mouthful would be painful, I discovered a whole half of banana, an item of food far too rare in my experience. I was provoked with myself because I was too full to eat, but I resolved that I would return for it after the meeting.

The more I reflected on the wealth of food before me, the more I felt the need of peace with the creatures who supplied it.

As a result of my hearty appetite, I was a trifle late in reaching the balcony, and the place was already overflowing with nervous mouse folk. Below, a large number of people had already assembled. Wisemouse and I both tried to appear calm. But I couldn't help feeling proud as I looked down at the work on the blackboard, which I pointed out to the mouse folk about me. "I guess they're all here," said Wisemouse, as the same man person we saw before rose to speak. We were breathless, but I was also disappointed because the people had not noticed my work.

"Their eyes are not as good as ours," said Wisemouse, trying to comfort me. However, we were not to be disappointed for long.

Hardly had the man person started speaking than a woman person gave a loud shriek.

"Look," she cried hysterically pointing to the blackboard. "The mice have written to us!" As if terrified, the whole audience rose up and rushed to the blackboard. What they said of course I learned only through Wisemouse.

"Nonsense!" exclaimed the man when the noise subsided. "Even school mice can't read and write. Someone is playing a joke on us." However his words had no calming effect. The people wanted to believe in us.

"Wouldn't it be thrilling," exclaimed one woman, "if we really could talk to mice? What interesting stories they could tell us! I, myself, never was afraid of them. Let us write them and see if they answer us."

Some persons laughed nervously, but all were serious.

The man was very provoked and sounded

as if he were talking to very stupid young people. "It would be very nice, indeed, if we could talk to mice. Maybe we could invite them to the table to eat with us, and we could teach them table manners. I, for one, will believe it when I see them writing."

Everybody laughed.

While the man spoke, Wisemouse was silent. He was nervous and trembling. "That's what I was afraid of. They won't believe we wrote it."

Not till then did I realize this possible failure. All his wisdom and all my work was useless.

In my sudden panic, an awesome thought seized me—inspired by the man's words "when I see them writing." Hardly knowing what I did, I ran to the stairway and leaped down a whole step after step. Once in the big crowded hall I rushed to the wall, up the wainscoting to the chalk rail in front of what was now an excited throng of people. They suddenly backed away from the blackboard as hurriedly as they

had approached it a few moments before. Seizing the same piece of chalk I had used, I dragged it across the board in a straight line. With a flourish I led it to our message.

Then before the excited people could approach me I dropped to the floor, scurried out into the hall, up the back steps, and in a minute joined Wisemouse. And together with the excited, applauding mouse folk, we looked down on the turmoil I had created.

Wisemouse was trembling with excitement. "Moose, you were wonderful. But let's listen."

The man person was no longer talking, but he sat huddled up as if stunned. A lady person was standing in his place. "There is no question," she said, "that we have treated mice shamefully. All the time we did know that they drove crawling insects from our houses and also that they eat weed seeds. But too often we have overlooked our greatest debt to them: their contribution to medical science. Surely we should not begrudge them the food we throw away. If we feed them where we want them to be, they won't come where we don't want them to be. I, personally, will never set another trap."

Elated even as we now were, we mouse folk were thunderstruck at the applause below us when the person took a seat. Wisemouse could hardly speak. "We were very wise not to threaten them. It's fear that brings on wars."

We mouse folk lingered long after the confused, noisy people left the building. The excited mice still surrounded me asking all kinds of questions and extolling my courage. As I started to leave, Wisemouse spoke to me with great emotion:

"Moose," he said, "we must not be too hopeful. People are warring creatures by nature. They have always been fighting among themselves—even when there is enough food for everyone. In fact, they seem to consider fighting a privilege. They always stand aside and let their young go to war first. Every other creature I know of makes its young stay at home."

Suddenly, while Wisemouse was speaking, I was aware that Miss Whitemouse was near me and was looking at me in a way that made me feel very self-conscious. The next moment I was utterly unnerved as she impulsively pressed her nose against mine. "Moose," she said softly, "you are the bravest mouse that ever lived."

I was so flustered that the only words I could say had nothing to do with what we had been discussing.

"You are the most beautiful mouse in the world."

And I, who had defied a fierce cannibal cat, thundering automobiles, and hundreds of people, actually trembled.

It was not until long after midday, when I was in bed at home, that I remembered the half banana I had left in the schoolhouse basement. I fully realized that this tragic lapse of memory was all the fault of Miss Whitemouse.

Yet I was not a bit angry with her.